Falling Out of the Sky

POEMS ABOUT MYTHS AND MONSTERS

Edited by Rachel Piercey and Emma Wright

With poems from John Canfield, Mary Anne Clark, Joseph Coelho, Sarah Doyle, Matt Goodfellow, Matt Haigh, John Fuller, Anna Kisby, Harry Man, Amy McCauley, Paul McMenemy, Rachael M Nicholas, Richard O'Brien, Abigail Parry, Rachel Piercey, Lavinia Singer, Jon Stone, Kate Wakeling, Kate Wise and Andrew Wynn Owen

Illustrated by Emma Wright

THE EMMA PRESS
CHILDREN'S BOOKS

ACKNOWLEDGEMENTS

'Siren', by Amy McCauley, was first published in The Rialto
(Issue 70: Autumn 2014)

'At Home with the Witch from Hansel and Gretel' by
Har... ...by b. Bruce...
House' on...

THE EMMA PRESS

First published in Great Britain in 2015
by the Emma Press Ltd

ISBN 978-1-910139-18-9

A CIP catalogue record of this book
is available from the British Library.

Printed and bound in Great Britain
by TJ International Ltd, Padstow, Cornwall

theemmapress.com
queries@theemmapress.com

CONTENTS

∞

Introduction

It's a very human instinct to want to tell stories. Since the start of humankind we have told stories to try and make sense of the world, asking and answering *How did the universe begin? Why are we here? Is there more to life than what we can see?*

We tell stories to explain our origins and those of the plants, animals, weather and heavens. We tell stories to feed our curiosity about why bad things happen and what lies beyond our life on earth.

We also tell each other about amazing things that have happened. We rejoice in the achievements of extraordinary people, and we whisper cautionary tales about people who were too proud or greedy or foolish. Some stories change in the telling, taking on embellishments so that, over time, true things can seem like invention and nobody is sure what really happened.

Good stories, whether true or invented, will be told and retold. Myths and legends can endure for thousands of years, as long as people keep hearing them and wanting to pass them on. The poets in *Falling Out of the Sky* have chosen to retell some of their favourite stories about heroes, villains, monsters and gods, taking inspiration from and adding their own twists to stories originally told in ancient Greece, Mexico, Wales, Scandinavia, Indonesia, Turkey, Germany, Italy and England. This book contains just a tiny fraction of all the myths and legends out there in the world, and Rachel (Piercey, my co-editor) and I hope these poems will encourage you to go and find your own favourites.

We also hope you might start to spot some of the stories and names from this book in other places – in other books, poems, television shows, comics, films, paintings, drawings, video games, and even conversations. People often draw on older stories when telling new ones, and it can be fun to spot the older story hovering in the background and to think about why it's there. Some of the characters and events might even stick with you so much that you start to use them when you're telling your own stories!

Emma Wright
WINNERSH
June 2015

Falling Out of the Sky

Poems about Myths and Monsters

The Minotaur was half man and half bull.

King Minos of
Crete kept the
Minotaur in the
Labyrinth,
a complex maze
designed by an
inventor called
Daedalus
(see page 101).

THE MINOTAUR

Rachael M Nicholas

In the middle of the middle of a dark, dark maze
lived the monstrous Minotaur.

He had two sharp horns and fearsome teeth
and a deep and horrible roar.

No one should have to go in there,
in the dark with that terrible beast

but fourteen young men and young women
were sent in for the monster to feast.

Then, with his sword, came Theseus,
who had heard of the young people's plight.

He promised to enter the Labyrinth
and challenge the fiend to a fight.

Ariadne, the King's clever daughter,
knew a sword wasn't enough,

getting in to the maze would be easy,
but getting out again, that would be tough.

The Labyrinth was built to be tricky,
to bewilder and trap and mislead,

Ariadne knew Theseus needed her help
if his plan was to ever succeed.

So she gave him a ball of red-coloured string
and told him to use it with care,

to tie one end tight at the start of the maze
before entering the Minotaur's lair.

Round each darkened bend and each miserable pass
crept Theseus, sword in his hand,

and he unwound the string he'd been given,
as smart Ariadne had planned.

At last he came to the middle,
and the Minotaur came in to view,

and Theseus, shaking but ready,
did what he had promised to do.

He fought with the beast in the darkness,
till the Minotaur fell down dead,

and then Theseus retraced each step he had made,
following the line of the thread.

It takes more than a sword to slay monsters.
Without bravery a sword's just a thing,

and let's not forget Ariadne,
with her plan and her ball of red string.

ख

You can read more about the Minotaur on page 86.

Ginny Green Teeth is also known as 'Jenny Greenteeth'.

Ginny Green Teeth

Matt Goodfellow

Ginny Green Teeth is hiding in the water,
Ginny Green Teeth is the Devil's own daughter.

Out among the shallows of the boggy Cheshire plain,
underneath the duckweed, there's a demon that's a-laying,
waiting for a wanderer to step too close and then
they're pulled into the underworld and never seen again.

Ginny Green Teeth is hiding in the water,
Ginny Green Teeth is the Devil's own daughter.

Children of the villages are warned to never play
anywhere near marshy ground or swampy waterway.
When moonlight on the sniddlebog is shining clear and cold,
the water-wench is prowling, on the hunt for careless souls.

Ginny Green Teeth is hiding in the water,
Ginny Green Teeth is the Devil's own daughter.

☙

the heavens

the skies

the weather

the animals

the plants

the planets

the underworld

the stars

everything else

Different cultures have different beliefs and stories to explain how the world began and how everything else started...

The Serpent and the Turtle

Kate Wakeling

Now, if you lie an ear to the earth
you'll hear it had many beginnings:
beginnings that began with birds or bridges
or ice or eggs or you-name-it,
someone will tell you a story that starts with it.

So, here is one such beginning to the world
from the small, green island of Bali
and it is certainly a good 'un.
Or, as a Balinese person might say:
eyyyyy, bechik-bechik.

At this beginning of the world
there was not too much of anything
(as is often the case).
There was only a flat, single nothing
which was all at once the
longest-shortest-clearest-
cloudiest-sweetest-sourest-nothingest
nothing that ever there was.

Or rather, wasn't.

And in the middle of this nothing
there lived a snakey, serpenty
slitherer called Antaboga.
(You can rhyme Antaboga with *Rant! A frog jar!*
but I suggest you don't.)
Antaboga the serpent had a slipping,
sliding rainbow belly
and he was as long as a story with no end
but twice as lonely.

One morning, Antaboga decided it was about time
there was less *nothing*
and more *something*.

So this is what he did:
Antaboga closed his cool, black eyes
and fell into a long, low snooze
that bid his blood to doze in his veins,
while deep inside his green and serpenty brains
he began to dream of a

    t   u   r   t   l   e   .   .   .

a turtle so huge, so high,
so mind-janglingly enormous
that even the tiniest tooth
at the back of the turtle's great green mouth
was twenty-two times taller
than the mightiest mountain you could imagine.

And just like that, the turtle appeared,
for this is how things were done in those days.

The turtle's name was Bedwang
(which is said just as you want to say it)
and Bedwang (correct!) also agreed it was about time
there was less nothing
and more something.

Better yet, Bedwang the turtle had an idea.

He realised his huge, green shell
was the perfect place to put
islands and oceans and songs and gongs
and people and pineapples,
by which Bedwang meant

e   v   e   r   y   t   h   i   n   g

and no sooner had Bedwang the turtle
begun to imagine
islands and oceans and songs and gongs
and people and pineapples
balanced on his shell,
then just like that, they appeared,
for this is how things were done in those days.
There was, however, a problem.

When everything had settled on Bedwang's back,
Bedwang found he had a fidget in his front left foot
and try as he might not to fidget,

                                fidget he did,

and the instant he twitched
so the world above him twitched
and the ocean bellowed and the ground trembled
and Bedwang saw that he'd better be careful,
for no one wants bellows or trembles like those.
But as everybody knows,
a fidget can be tricky to refuse.

And so it came to pass
that Antaboga the serpent and Bedwang the turtle
had made the world and given it a home,
and while Bedwang slept and twitched
and twitched and slept
(which meant the world on his back
slept and twitched and twitched and slept),
still Antaboga and his rainbow belly
drifted on beyond the skies,
as long as a story with no end
but now twice as cheerful.

And that, dear reader,
is how this particular beginning
began.

℞

Pandora's Box

Andrew Wynn Owen

Zeus was in his study,
skimming over e-mails,
browsing wedding gifts to
 order for a friend:
'Teapots look outdated,
cushions are too kitsch, and
people who give vouchers
 drive me round the bend.

Hey, Pandora's fun – I'm
sure she would adore a
box containing all the
    world's potential ills!
Yes, that's what I'll get her.
Let's see, maybe there's one
hidden under all these
    unpaid lightning bills.'

At the wedding, Zeus swanned
over, said, 'Don't open –
tricky to explain, but
    evil lies within!'
Adding, 'Don't you dare to
say I didn't warn you!
('Grats on getting hitched.)' He
    vanished with a grin.

Curiosity's a
tantalising thrill of
life. I guess Pandora
    knew she couldn't keep
back forever from the
box. Had she not winched it
open then, she would have
    done it in her sleep.

Dear Pandora, darling,
heaven knows, if only
you'd restrained your hand, how
    perfect Earth might be:
nonstop jubilation,
barbecues and banquets!
But that's not what went down
    in mythology.

Aggravations, issues,
itchinesses, dangers,
stinging nettles, hornets
    burst out from the box
like a pressure mounting
underneath the lid, all
eager to escape and
    chafing at the locks.

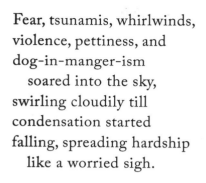

Fear, tsunamis, whirlwinds,
violence, pettiness, and
dog-in-manger-ism
   soared into the sky,
swirling cloudily till
condensation started
falling, spreading hardship
   like a worried sigh.

Naiads, dryads, satyrs
playing golf and frisbee
suddenly were plagued by
   an appalling pong.
'Why are all the roses,'
wailed a shepherd, 'wilting?
Surely in Arcadia
   nothing can go wrong?'

Maybe you can picture
how distressed our hero
kind Pandora felt to
   see what she'd set off.
Who could bear to think that
all this planet's woes were
started by oneself, from
   war to whooping cough?

Hang on! What's that glinting
in the box's corner?
Dora saw a sight that
    heartened her to cope:
crushed beneath the weight of
every hellish horror
lay another force: the
    name of this was 'Hope'!

Hope arose, resplendent,
green as spring and grinning
impishly: Pandora
    suddenly felt strong
as she recognised a
force beyond all others,
fitting in like it had
    been there all along.

Hope's a party guest who's
never uninvited,
Hope's a leprechaun who
    hollers, 'All is well!'
Hope's a multi-purpose
giver of advice, and
hope's a tortoise armoured
    safely in its shell.

Hope's the one emotion
needed to feel happy;
nothing else will win when
    hope is in the ring.
Hope's for now-and-always,
hope's our atmosphere, and
hope's the reason every
    optimist can sing.

಄

Odysseus was an ancient Greek hero who fought in the Trojan War and afterwards took a very long time to get back home.

Odysseus met several monsters on his way home to Ithaca, including the one-eyed Cyclops, the witch Circe and the irresistible Sirens...

Siren Song

Rachel Piercey

Sirens! The cry went round the ship
as swift as if they'd sighted home
and every sailor felt the grip

of fear and gathered in a throng,
for no man can resist the song
of sirens luring them to come,

and run their ships into the rocks
by chasing the enchanted tones.
Tie me! cried Odysseus,

Here are ropes, the mast is strong;
now bind me tight so I may hear
the rapture of the spells they cast

and yet be helpless to respond;
then plug this beeswax in your ears
and we'll be safe from siren song!

The ship sailed hesitantly past
the outcrop where the sirens lay,
and each one skimmed her voice across

the waves, and each voice crept and slid
and whispered to Odysseus:
Oh captain, turn your ship our way

and you will have your heart's desire,
for we know everything there is
of gods and men, of land and sky,

and every deed that's been and done
and every deed that is to come...
And if you join us, you will live!

Odysseus raged against his ties
and screamed at his unhearing men,
beseeched and threatened with his eyes

for them to cut him free to steer
the ship towards the sirens' cries –
for the sirens promised him the world

and then he could go home again.
But the men obeyed his first command
and tied more ropes with shaking hands

and pulled the oars and prayed the wind
would fill the sail and move them clear
and soon they left the rocks behind.

Their captain calmed as they sailed on
and soon he signalled with a frown
that they should free him from the mast

and all the sailors cheered to think
theirs was the only ship to pass
the sirens and not break and sink!

Odysseus lent his voice to theirs
and told them how the sirens sang
and every sailor laughed and drank,

hailing the gods and giving thanks.
And in the hubbub no one saw
Odysseus growing pale and grieved,

or how he pressed his ringing ears,
or how he kept himself withdrawn,
his eyes fixed on the rills of foam

that flowed behind the merry boat,
as if he longed for what was gone.
Oh captain, turn your ship our way

and you will have your heart's desire,
for we know everything there is
of gods and men, of land and sky,

and every deed that's been and done
and every deed that is to come…

No one is safe from siren song.

☙

Odysseus was famous
for his cunning plans.
He was the one who
suggested building the
Trojan Horse, which
helped the Greeks to
win the war against
the Trojans. This is
the horse which Epeius
(on page 77) built.

Some myths explain aspects of the natural world. This next poem is based on an Aztec myth explaining how the moon came to exist, and why it is covered in craters.

LORD OF THE SNAILS

Anna Kisby

I

I wanted to be the SUN. I wanted to fly up to the sky, hang there in flames. I was too slow. I dragged my foot. Couldn't make up my mind which way to go. The wild gods slapped me, dimmed me, left me with scars. I became the MOON.

am Lord of the Snails

❦

ARACHNOPHOBIA

Kate Wise

Arachne was a weaver
but cursed with terrible pride.
'Even a goddess can do no better!
I'm the best there is!' she cried.

Athena heard her from the skies
and thought, 'I've heard enough!
Who is this mortal who dares to boast?
I'll challenge her to a weave-off.'

A rule of thumb:
Don't wind the gods up.
It doesn't usually end well...

Arachne wove as well as ever;
silks fine as thistle-puff.
But against the gods, simply clever
just isn't good enough.

Athena wove sunbeams, starlight,
dancing waves from sapphire seas,
green whispers of the summer grass,
red deaths of autumn leaves.

Arachne lost. Her punishment?
She's there for you to see:
on the cobwebbed kitchen ceiling
she spins eternally.

☙

In Greek myths,
humans were
often punished for
daring to challenge
the gods. Turn to
page 57 to see what
happened to poor
Marsyas.

Athena was the Greek goddess of wisdom, justice and the arts.

Francis of Assisi was an Italian friar who was made a saint after his death. He is known as the patron saint of animals.

St Francis and
the Wolf of Gubbio

John Fuller

Little Brother Francis, you have performed many miracles.
Can you save us here in Gubbio from the frightful wolf
Who patrols our town like a landlord or a sentry?

Its breath is foul and black
As a pit dug for the plague
And all along its back
Stand the stumps of old arrows.

No one can catch it! No one can kill it!
The mayor runs whimpering to his bedroom
And the baby is snatched up from the doorway!

Wolf? Wolf? Are you there?
Where are you, wolf?

The lights burn at the empty feast.
Windows are bolted like loaded guns
And the hour comes when the beast
Of all our desires and ill wishes
Pads up and down in the moonlight.

Wolf, are you there? Where are you, wolf?
Come to Brother Francis. Come and lick my hand.

The blackness gives back the echo of fear.
A mouth with teeth behind every wall.
A slavering jaw waiting to make its entry.
Not there! Here! Over here! Behind you!

Come to Brother Francis. Come and lick my hand.
There shall be no fear or anger in any creature.
I can look in his eye and he can look into mine.
The wolf in me sees the man in him
And fears no more, knowing
That nature may be pacified.

Through that eye, that dark centre
No bigger than a scorch on linen
When the cinder is brushed away
As soon as it leaps from the fire,
Through his wicked eye I can see his soul,
And the devil in it leaps out, crying:
'Wolf! You have betrayed me!'

Now heads turn back to their plumped-up pillows.
And the streets are quiet in the cradle of the starlight.

ଔ

This is the Cornish legend of Saint Senara and her son Saint Budoc.

Saint Senara and Me

Anna Kisby

We're floating away in a barrel,
Princess Senara and me.

The malevolent King packed us in,
hurled us into the Celtic sea.

Selkies sing to us, porpoises guide us,
kittiwakes point the way.

Senara rows with her strong arms
and feeds me turtle tea.

She reads the stars, she whispers to waves,
she calms their swell and gyre.

She keeps me warm in her long red hair
tangled with langoustines.

We pitch and roll, I swallow the rain,
our barrel fills with minnows.

Senara grows gills and a silvery tail,
she swims us into tomorrow.

The Bay of Biscay is far away,
my toes touch shingle and shale.

I crawl onto the sand of this tin-rich land,
saved by my mermaid mother.

CR

THE FURIES

Lavinia Singer

Beneath the earth they wait   hissing
Deep in graves of dirt   listening
Blood-red eyes of hate   dripping

Each faithless man they take in turn
The violent husbands, liars, thieves
Ruled by lust, desire or greed
Are captured, never to return

With wings of bats unrolled   beating
Their skin is black as coal   glistening
Skulls with serpents coiled   shrieking

Torches, daggers, whips and knives
Teeming cups of poisoned drink
Nightmares issue from each wink
Justice is repaid with life

The vengeful sisters wait   unceasing
Administering their rage   believe it
So think before you play   or trick me

The Furies were the ancient Greek goddesses of vengeance.

The Ballad of Echo and Narcissus

Sarah Doyle

There lived a girl in Ancient Greece
who sought the perfect man.
A mate on whom to lavish love,
and so her search began.
Fair Echo was the maiden's name
and she was quite a catch:
she had her pick of suitors who
might be the ideal match.

Now, Echo was the choosy sort
and she had set her cap
at someone named Narcissus,
who was quite a dishy chap.
Good looking, yes. But modest? No.
Narcissus was the kind
who didn't let his handsomeness
stray too far from his mind.

Echo was a nymph who had been cursed by the goddess Hera to be able to speak only what someone else had just said – that is, to echo them. In this poem, Echo is allowed to squeeze out a few of her own words.

He loved himself, Narcissus did,
far more than words can say.
Unless you held a mirror up,
he wouldn't look your way.
So this was lonely Echo's choice:
a man who lived to preen.
But when she bared her soul to him,
he said 'I'm not that keen.'

'For why would I look on your face,
when easily in sight
are my own charming features
which enthral, bewitch, delight?'
Without the smallest conscience-prick,
Narcissus, the upstart,
rejected Echo out of hand
and broke her fragile heart.

She wept all day, she wept all night,
much wailing in the mix.
Poor Echo, she wept buckets,
fit to flood the River Styx.
Upon this scene of howling grief,
there entered Nemesis.
'My dear,' she said, 'may I be told
just what the matter is?'

'You're sat there crying like a babe,
a female fountain spout.
Come, tell your Aunty Nemesis –
let all your troubles out.'
'Oh Nemesis, oh Nemesis,
I've such a dismal lot.
Narcissus doesn't love me!'
wailed sad Echo, through the snot.

Well, Nemesis was quite enraged
on our poor girl's behalf:
'He loves himself too much, that one.
I'll have the final laugh!'
She thundered on: 'The boy's a chump.
A blockhead. It's his loss.
That vain, conceited imbecile –
I'll show him who's the boss!'

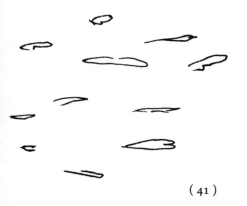

People nowadays sometimes refer to their enemy as their 'nemesis'. In Greek mythology, Nemesis was a goddess who made sure everyone got their just deserts and punished those who became too proud.

(Like all good gods and goddesses,
she never was averse
to doling out some punishment
or casting the odd curse.)
She found Narcissus soon enough –
ignoring his appeals,
she cursed him so he'd clock his face
and fall head over heels.

So down beside the riverbank,
Narcissus chanced upon
his face reflecting up at him –
and he was solid gone.
'Ye Gods, but I am gorgeous, though!'
the vain Narcissus cried.
'If I were food, I'd eat myself,
right by this riverside.'

Narcissus, thus afflicted,
couldn't tear himself away;
and rooted by the riverbank,
he passed each night and day.
Old Nemesis, that vengeful queen,
felt really rather smug
to see Narcissus on his knees,
obsessed with his own mug.

Refusing food, refusing drink,
refusing all affection
that loyal Echo offered him,
he gazed at his reflection.
And naturally, it wasn't long
until the finish came.
Narcissus ailed, then changed into
the bloom that bears his name.

Now have your hankies close to hand
as, though it's sad to tell,
this being Greek mythology,
it doesn't end that well.

You may assume, now Echo had seen
mean Narcissus wilt,
that she'd be full of triumph,
but all Echo felt was guilt.

She missed her would-be boyfriend
and she still bemoaned her fate.
No man to love, no hand to hold,
no weekend dinner-date.
Poor Echo's anguish cut so deep,
she couldn't leave the place
where silly boy Narcissus
had once idolised his face.

So, like all love-lorn heroines,
the lonely Echo pined
and left, for those who care to hear,
her legacy behind.
For Echo loved Narcissus so,
she never could rejoice.
She faded, till there just remained
her voice, her voice, her voice...

ᠻᢒ

SIREN

Amy McCauley

You who listen hear me.
You who place your ear against this space,
which sometimes only seems unseemingly
to listen, listen.

You who listen, hear me.
You who have a mind to have an ear for what is wordless,
let me pare you down to just an ear
and I will sing.

You who listen, hear me.
I sing you in slowly; slowly I sing you in.
How easy it is to move you.
Now you are swimming.

☙

In Greek mythology, the
Sirens were creatures
whose beautiful voices
lured sailors to their
doom on jagged rocks.

(45)

There are many
stories about
people making
pacts with or
selling their soul
to the devil.
There is always
a catch and it
usually ends
badly!

The Legend of
Jan Tregeagle

John Canfield

Beyond the River Tamar, to the west –
when all the miner's wheelhouses still turn
and stand porth-proud, an age before their waste,
the ground beneath them filled with golden tin –

this county, Cornwall, hosts a magistrate,
a steward, lawyer, landlord, six feet tall;
a swindler, thief, a liar and a cheat;
and those he cannot steal from, he will kill.

He robs an orphan of inheritance;
the farmers on his land work twice as hard;
as magistrate, there can be no defence
against his judgements, cruel to young and old.

He marries heiresses, and one by one
he murders them, inheriting their gold –
though this is not enough: it's said by some
he meets the devil, selling him his soul.

Tower-tall with burning eyes,
arms that stretch out forty-span,
lips that only spit out lies,
Tregeagle is a wicked man.

But soon, he sees his life will not last long;
the devil will take back what he now owns.
Tregeagle bribes the clergy, when he's gone,
to bury him within the church's grounds.

The day comes when Tregeagle joins the dead.
The clergy – with a freshly brimming purse –
now do the duty for which they've been paid,
but all too late: he will not rest in peace.

Tower-tall with burning eyes,
arms that stretched out forty-span,
lips that only spat out lies,
Tregeagle was a wicked man.

Not long after, a debtor is in court:
a moneylender gave this man a loan,
the scoundrel is denying it – he thought
the only witness to it was long gone.

Tregeagle was the one who saw the deal,
and now he's dead, the foolish man cries 'Ef
Tregeagle seed the money paid, then he'll
appear here from his grave to show the proof!'

A bolt of lightning flashes round the room:
Tregeagle stands before them cloaked in rage.
'You found et plain to bring me here, but you
will find et hard to send me back again.'

Tregeagle leaps to tear him limb from limb;
the coward panics, grabs a newborn child,
holds it aloft – and innocence saves him;
a clergyman orders the ghost outside.

Tower-tall with burning eyes,
arms that stretch out forty-span,
the grave won't keep him where he lies:
Tregeagle is a wicked man.

With shrieks, he flees to Roche Rock where he sees
a chapel; following the sound of bells,
this evil spirit seeks out sanctuary
but cannot fit inside; he stands and howls.

The vicar bids him on to Bodmin Moor
but cannot send his spirit back to hell,
so sets a task to last forevermore
and gives him just a leaking limpet shell

and orders him to drain Dozmary Pool,
a lake they say is bottomless; his fate
an endless task befitting one so cruel;
demons from hell torment him, day and night.

Tower-tall with burning eyes,
at night, when on the Moor, you can
still hear the awful, tortured cries
come from Tregeagle, wretched man.

છ

Terrainiac, otherwise known as Tlaloc

A Rowdy Bunch of Rough and Tumble Aztec Gods

Abigail Parry and Jon Stone

TERRAINIAC THE RAIN GOD

Terrainiac's always wet through.
He shakes himself down, starts a storm or two.
Water whirls for miles. He shakes off snails
and snakes and frogs, then the jaggedy white trails
of lightning bolts. He shakes so frantically
the dead get up to clap and every tree
starts headbanging! Then, when he's done,
instead of drying himself out in the sun,
he squelches back to his cave in the mountain,
still drizzling like a broken fountain.

SKELETON DOG BOY

Skeleton Dog Boy!
Bloody-knees, long-bones,
loot-god, eel-knot,
stony dolt.

Skeleton Dog Boy!
Bent key, bone-boss,
knobbly sky-goon,
golden boy.

Skeleton Dog Boy!
Soot god, blood god,
snot-nosed yob-god,
lost boy, nobody.

Skeleton Dog Boy, otherwise known as Xolotl

Flower Prince and Monkey, otherwise
known as Xochipilli and Ozotmatli (right)

FLOWER PRINCE AND MONKEY

Flower Prince daydreams in his favourite chair.
He's gorged on treats and coffee. There's a tear
in the sky above him,
and the sun has begun to swim.
Monkey's asleep on the roof. The two of them
love dice and cards and every other game.
They like to play at rhyme,
chase girls, be chased by girls, and climb
up trees to spy on all the parties all across the world.
They're terribly skilled
at trickery, and love to trick mean men.
They stay up late and do it all again!
But all that playing soon leaves them exhausted,
dazed and dusted.
The lazy sun watches
them lie down to dream, two little burnt matches.

VOLCANO-GLASS BUTTERFLY

Two bat-black wings –
each wing
is tipped with a knife
and she clacks and clicks
when she flaps
like a bag of plastic bricks,
rook-black, and glossy
like a truncheon,
shiny as a scorpion!
Hot like lava!
Out all night,
making sure
all the monsters behave
and don't leave their lairs
and never
go bothering children.

Tussocky Hairdo, or Zacatzontli

Volcano-Glass Butterfly, or Itzpapalotl

TUSSOCKY HAIRDO

Tussocky Hairdo sleeps in the day
and jumps up, his tussocky hair in disarray,
every night. His job's to patrol
the darkest, snakiest roads where travellers stroll.
He knows that roads at night are sly. They slip
from under you or lead you round in a loop.
So Tussocky Hairdo goes to keep them pinned
with feathers from his bag of birds. The wind
runs through his tussocky hair
and carries him almost everywhere.

THE LAMENT OF RABBIT-FACED MOONMAN

Look at him, that big show-off,
the Sun! All because he was brave enough
to jump on a bonfire. Ugh.

Meanwhile, I hang here, disgraced.
Lilywhite and tremulous,
this rabbit shaming my face.

☙

You can
read another
poem about
Rabbit-Faced
Moonman
(Tecciztecatl)
on page 26.

Apollo Comes to Town

Richard O'Brien

I don't mean to be rude in saying
   Phrygia was the pits.
Some dead towns come to life at night,
   but this one got more stiff
(and if a place could have two faces,
   this one wasn't it).

There wasn't much to get young Phrygians
   up and out of bed –
a draper's shop, Subway, a rock,
   and a Phrygian launderette.
(It took two weeks to clock the fact
   the draper had dropped dead.)

In short, there wasn't much you could call
   'cultural heritage'.
So pity Marsyas, who lived
   in the back side of the Phryg',
with half-eaten bananas, beans,
   and other things that squidge.

This Marsyas was a hairy sort.
  He didn't shave. He shambled.
He liked his eggs the way his head
  could not help being – scrambled –
and bits of them stuck in his beard,
  like wax dried round a candle.

But Marsyas was perking up,
  'cause Marsyas had found
a way out of his dirty, no-good,
  stinking Phrygian town –
his flute. He gave a hirsute toot
  and let the notes resound,

and from all corners of the town,
     crowds came. They left their cars
abandoned on the one road out;
     they left their doors ajar.
They'd never known a thing like this –
     a home-grown Phrygian star!

Now, I'm not saying Marsyas' music
     was the best thing on the air
(though even that was stale and dirty).
     Ladies' underwear
did not descend on his crescendoes,
     and his clothes were square,
but here's the thing: when you've got
     nothing else, you *care*.

You care, if for no other reason
     than your Phrygian pride,
about this schlub, so painfully
     ill-equipped to change the tide,
because he might be square and hairy,
     but at least he's on *our side*.

At least, that is, of course, until
    Apollo comes to town,
in his big tour-bus with its tinted windows
    rolled a quarter down,
so all you can see's one godlike eyebrow,
    the hint of a holy frown.

And when Apollo came to town,
    he was instantly accosted.
The Phrygians swarmed his tour bus
    like they planned to take him hostage
– queued up for selfies, gave him the town keys,
    basically Phrygia lost it.

Apollo was the Greek
god of music, prophecy,
medicine, the sun... and
poetry.

You should have seen the surge
　　　when he deigned to emerge
　with his lyre and his golden quiff,
as he raised his arms in his singlet top
　　and gave each armpit a sniff,
before smiling and waving;
　　　then stopped in his tracks.
　The way a bad smell drifts,

a sound had drifted into his orbit,
　　a note, a tentative trill,
like a boy at his recorder practice,
　　getting to grips with the skill –
it was cute. It was charming. He found it alarming,
　　a challenge. It had to be killed.

Soon the word went like smoke
　　　through the Phrygian folk:
　Apollo would never play there
until all competition
　　　was flogged to submission.
　They brought Marsyas to the square.
He was clutching his flute
　　　in a double-denim suit,
　with catkins caught up in his hair.

The rules of the contest were simple:
 they each had a minute to play.
A panel of judges – we'll call them the Muses –
 sat silent, gave nothing away,
their facial expressions as empty and flat
 as a Phrygian nightclub on Friday.

Marsyas went first. If the coin-toss was rigged,
 I said nothing. I didn't speak.
The eyes of the crowd
  burnt him into the ground.
 He was earnest, and warbling, and weak,
when followed by Apollo's own
 immaculate technique.
Apollo socked the Muses into next week.

The Muses were the nine
goddesses of artistic and
scientific inspiration in
Greek mythology.

Inevitably then,
   all nine lights went green –
what a flawless performance!
   You made it your own!
With a voice like a god (well, exactly)
   and only nineteen!

And what about Marsyas,
   shambling and hairy?
An early retirement?
   A job in a dairy,
a life looking back on those
   fifteen short minutes of glory?

I'm afraid that's not quite
    how it works in this business.
The winner decides what the loser
    should get. This
is what he decided. It's tough,
    but the truth, kid,

is blades ripping down through
    the hide of our Phrygian,
dividing his skin from his
    inner vermillion
organs. Imagine a frog finding out
    that he's not an amphibian –

that was how Marsyas
    looked in the square,
with his flayed outer layer
    just hanging limply there;
a pool of blood reaming
    a dropped skirt of hair
while Apollo sat beaming,
    still playing the lyre.

Poor Marsyas, parted from
    all he held dear,
with his heart, lungs and liver
    exposed to the air
and his flute snapped in two
    rolling red on the floor
and Apollo just sitting there,
    playing the lyre.

ⓒ℞

To Asgard!

Rachel Piercey

*Come across the rainbow bridge
to Asgard, where the Norse gods live!*

Odin is the ruler here,
he strokes his beard, he shakes his spear,
he keeps a pair of wolves as pets
and flies a horse who has eight legs.

Come across the rainbow bridge
to Asgard, where the Norse gods live!

Frigg is queen, and she can see
what every person's fate will be,
and whether it will turn out well
or badly, though she'll never tell.

Come across the rainbow bridge
to Asgard, where the Norse gods live!

The strongest of them all is Thor
whose hammer causes thunderstorms.
He crushes mountains, likes to flirt,
has two goats pull his cart to work.

Come across the rainbow bridge
to Asgard, where the Norse gods live!

Freya's husband roams the worlds,
so she cries tears of solid gold.
In feathered cloak, boar at her side,
she goes to seek him far and wide.

Come across the rainbow bridge
to Asgard, where the Norse gods live!

Loki is the trickster god:
he causes trouble, then he's off,
and even Odin cannot make
this wily, wicked god behave.

*Come across the rainbow bridge
to Asgard, where the Norse gods live!*

Their world is full of beasts and swords,
serpents, giants, magic wars.
They feast and fight and feast again
but even Asgard has to end...

*So while there's still a rainbow bridge:
to Asgard! where the Norse gods live...*

❧

Turn to page 104 to find out what happens when Asgard
does come to an end.

The Welsh witch Ceridwen was brewing a potion to turn her foolish son handsome and wise...

THE CAULDRON OF KNOWLEDGE

Matt Haigh

Gwion Bach, come back, brat. My cauldron is cold
and the broth it brews is inside you!
That potion's gold, you've no clue – you'll be stewed
to porridge by its knowledge.
I'll catch you; I'm no old goat,
my greyhound eyes fixed on your throat.

Ceridwen, you're a clueless hen.
As for your wrath – now I'm a hare
out-bounding your pot-bellied puppy shape
while you scrape the barrel of taste.
Your flea-bitten form's a waste.
I'm gone, I'm off,
your knowledge is mine, you've lost.
Go stomp at the gods.

Dross! Enough of this mutt,
on your bones I'll glut as I transform
by the brook to a beast who feasts on meat
(specifically sneaks who cheat and cheeks of churlish
boys) – a croc with crunching jaws,
my lunch will be your paws.

O wench, winch your body along –
catching me will be no cinch,
I'm a bird now, witch.
Watch me whip clouds to clown hair
while you itch to rip me to bits.
Talons outmatch
scalloped gallons of 'gator.
See you later.

Bird? Absurd! I'll smash you to sparrow-curd.
This cumbersome coat of scales I'll shed
then flense your flesh with my deft
and deadly eagle beak. Yes,
I'll catch you, cleave your carcass clean.
You think me mean? I'll churn you to cream.

Ceridwen, curdle-brain. Fast as flame
I'll beat you again. Feathers be gone
as I drop in a pond, a carp
cajoling in foam. That'll stopper
your plans, you walnut-witted rotter.
Give up. Don't bother.
I'm a flash of quicksilver,
a dream in water.

Little fish, you've quips and mirth to madden
but you'll smirk less when I change
to a dragon half-combusting with rage.
Prattle on, boy. You know I'll win.
One sneeze and my nostrils whip-
lash flame enough to sizzle fish to crisps.

Ceridwen, you'll be blighted.
I've heard dragons are short-sighted.
Flowers are surely too small to see –
my final form is decided.
Your goggles are too googly
to spot a tiny foxglove.
O vermillion me,
with knowledge now in love.

༄

As the story goes,
Ceridwen swallowed
Gwion and ended up
giving birth to him.
This baby would
become Taliesin, the
great 6th-century
Welsh poet.

Medusa and her sisters were
Gorgons, a kind of fearsome
monster in ancient Greek
mythology. They were said to
have snakes for hair and eyes
which could turn anyone
they looked at into stone.

Medusa and Her Sisters

Rachael M Nicholas

You can't wear a hat,
you can't plait your hair,
can't go swimming in lakes,
can't sleep well, can't sneak about,

but at least you're never alone
when your head is covered
in hissing,
        rustling,
                slithering
                        snakes.

My sisters say we're special.
They shake their heads, and
their snakes shake their heads,
and say I'm just being silly.

If I could see myself
in the mirror, they say,
without turning myself
into stone, I wouldn't feel
so sad.

So you can't wear a hat,
or plait your hair, or swim,
or sleep well, or sneak about.

So you turn people to stone
with one look. So what?

Everyone has to be something,
Medusa. Just be you, be just
as you are.

CR

Like Odysseus on page 21, Epeius fought in the Trojan War, which lasted ten years.

EPEIUS

Paul McMenemy

Once there was a man named Epeius.
He was not the wisest, or the smartest
(which is not the same thing),
or the kindest of men.
But he was the bravest.

Of all the Greeks to glower round Troy
he was the gloweringest.

He was first to any fisticuffs:
no job too large
or small.

As this is a children's book, I cannot describe for you
all the breezy bodyparts which billowed in his wake
as he swirled his sword through the Trojan horde.
You will have to imagine that for yourself.
But I can tell you he was brave.

Now, whether bravery is all it's cracked up to be
is another matter.
Is it better to be brave than smart?
Better to be brave than kind?
Better to be brave than wise?
Well, Epeius was brave.

And I can tell you something else:
he wasn't going in no horse, fool!

Now, this is an odd thing:
some people say Epeius built the Trojan Horse;
some people say the goddess Athene
came to him in a dream
and showed him how.

But let me ask you:
would a brave man hide in the hocks
of a heinous horse?
And slither down its wooden withers
whilst the trusting Trojans slept?

The Greeks spent nine years trying to break into the city of Troy. They finally managed it by pretending to go home but actually hiding inside a giant wooden horse. The Trojans wheeled the horse into their city because they thought was a farewell gift from the Greeks.

But Epeius was the bravest of the Greeks.
He was so brave that in years to come
whenever someone did something exceptionally brave
people would say, 'They're as brave as Epeius!'

When a boy leapt over a barrelling bull, they'd say,
'He's as brave as Epeius!'
When a girl stood up for her siblings at school,
they'd say, 'She's as brave as Epeius!'

But later, years later, so many years later
people would twist the phrase, as they do.
So when a boy leapt back
from a maundering mouse, they'd say,
'He's as brave as Epeius!'
When a girl stood on a silk-strumming spider,
they'd say, 'She's as brave as Epeius!'

Until later, years later, so many years later,
people forgot their own sarcasm, as they do.
And everyone knew
that Epeius was the greatest of the Greeks
for cowardice.

And when they came to tell the tale
of the Trojan horse, they'd say,
'That Epeius, that weasly, that shrinking Epeius –
that's exactly the kind of thing he would do!'

And now, years later, so many years later,
nobody remembers Epeius at all.

ℭℜ

PROMETHEUS
UNBOUND

Joseph Coelho

Rock-rooted regret,
liver-licked:
Prometheus is found
buried in eons of eagle droppings.
Face tanned by global warming,
skin sore from acid rain,
a film of pollutants dust him.

In the setting of night,
Prometheus hears
Heracles: the god-whisper, the body-thrum,
the muscle-hiss hero.

Heracles scales the mountain
wrapped in wrestled-lion fur,
hooded in tooth and claw.

Scars snake his body,
run up his neck,
frame his gold doe-eyes.

His arms pulse with the brawn of a boar,
his soiled hands have redirected rivers,
his fingers have flicked flight from feathers.

Heracles grins at Prometheus:
wild-stallion muscles twitching,
crazed-bull calves tensing,
eager for action,
giddy in the presence of this bright thief.

Heracles takes the binding chains and pulls...
snarling as his veins pop out,
twisting and surging
the god-sealed chains from the rock.

The eagle is heard before seen:
screech-wind, feather-tornado, claw-rain...

Heracles seizes its neck with one river-bed hand,
a beating wing with the other –
power floods his arms:
he pulls.
The eagle drops in two halves,
a dead feather-breath,
secretly relieved to be rid of the taste of liver.

Prometheus hears:
the god-whisper of a city,
the electric thrum of buildings,
the digital hiss of a new world.

છ

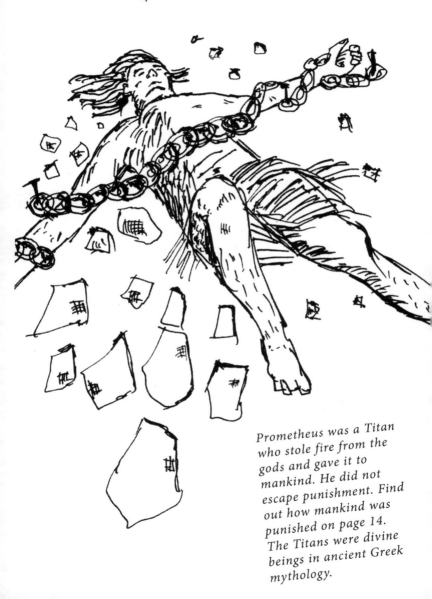

Prometheus was a Titan who stole fire from the gods and gave it to mankind. He did not escape punishment. Find out how mankind was punished on page 14. The Titans were divine beings in ancient Greek mythology.

LOVE SONG FOR
A MINOTAUR

Abigail Parry

You're lost, my love, you've lost your way,
I don't know how to find you now.
You tossed your head and went away,
the walls shot up and curved around –

a knot was tangled on the ground
and when you went, it slid and shut.
The walls shot up and curved around –
I can't get in, you can't get out.

A knot was tangled on the ground,
a knot was tangled in your heart.
The road was long and looped around
and hooked its ending to its start.

The road was long and looped around,
a riddle ran around its rim,
it slid and shut without a sound,
it shut me out, and shut you in.

A riddle is a tricksy thing –
it hooks its ending to its start.
I don't know how to work the string
that rigged a bloodknot in your heart.

I don't know how to work the string,
I don't know how to break the knot,
the heart is such a tricksy thing,
it shuts you in, or shuts you out.

A knot was tangled in your heart,
it tightened, tightened, every day.
I skipped around and played my part
but nothing I could do or say

could keep the road from curving round,
or turn your head, or break the day.
There is a riddle in the heart
that murmurs *go* when you should stay –

it shows you things you're dreaming of,
it picks them up and puts them down.
The world is full of monsters, love,
I don't think I can save you now.

The road curves on and on and on
with no way in, and no way out.
I couldn't follow. Now you're gone,
and no one else can reach you now.

☙

In Greek mythology, the Minotaur was a terrifying monster who lurked in the middle of a complex maze and ate Greek youths. Find out how the Minotaur met a grisly end on page 1.

Inspired by the German fairy tale.

At Home with the Witch from Hansel and Gretel

Harry Man

When I first moved in, I had to pinch myself. I used to wake up on Saturday mornings and say, 'Is this it? Am I really living in the countryside?' So from that point of view, the plot was a perfect find.

There's more involved than people think. Modern fixtures and fittings, and then this… my large Victorian aviary. It's about four times the size of an average Victorian bird cage, and it's probably the one feature of any room in the house that gets the most attention.

Typical double-glazing can be a bit boring, and in the end I went out on a limb. If you come a bit closer… here, touch the window… Now lick your finger, and again… what do you taste? Sugar! Exactly! Now tell me that's not the most amazing thing.

People come over all the time and they say how nice it looks. I say it will look a lot nicer when the beds have been dug in properly, and there's not so much wet jam everywhere. Upstairs is my room and the bathroom – en-suite of course... I am glad to be living in this part of the world. I've heard a lot of people around the New Forest use wheat straw thatching. I've used lime bootlaces. They keep the heat in and I think you'll agree, they add plenty of charm.

Come in and see the dining room... The walls here and throughout the house are built with a locally made gingerbread brick. This is my humbug table. As you can see it is made completely from humbugs. This is where all the atmosphere is – for me anyway. The house was a bit of an experiment, but I still wanted it to feel like a home... I like to think that's what I've achieved. These bobbly bits are flying saucers – you can give them a bit of a squeeze – so quite straightforward. It's really important to make it comfortable. If you put your mind to it, you can do all sorts.

Well I wanted a large oven because I like to have guests. Some people like a walk-in wardrobe, I like a walk-in oven. That's a German tiled chimney. We can take a look inside if you like, or would you and your friend like another look at the aviary?

Galahad the Good

Andrew Wynn Owen

Galahad, galloper,
son of Sir Lancelot,
best of the champions of
    Camelot's court –
how do you come to be
riding so late through a
forest, so far from a
    sheltering port?

My name, as you know, is Sir Galahad. I
    am the subject of many a tale.
By choice, I pursue an impractical aim:
    to find the Holy Grail.

Galahad, silver-sword,
heavens, I wasn't pre-
-pared to receive such an
          ardent reply!
Tell me, how long have you
been on the road, and then
if you've the time, please en-
          -lighten me why?

At Pentecost feast I sat down in a chair
          that Merlin had made to support
only the knight who could capture the Grail
          and carry it back to the court.

Galahad, spick-and-span,
all well and good, but it
sounds, as a job, like a
          bit of an ask.
What pre-existent ex-
-perience moved you to
think you were able and
          fit for the task?

Though brittler than angels, I'm more than a human
          because I believe in a zest
outside of this world but contained in all beings.
          This concentrates my quest.

Galahad, misty-eye,
what do you ponder when
scanning horizons as
        though they were ink?
When you stare out at a
sunset and whistle, what
scenes do you picture, what
        thoughts do you think?

I picture perpetually saints who meandered
        through history's corridors long
before I lived and laughed and learned
        what's right, and what is wrong.

Galahad, sleepy-head,
tell me, be honest, how
is it you manage to
        canter and keep
grip on a bridle and
foot in a stirrup when,
far as I see, you don't
        slacken to sleep?

I never can slow and I never can swerve
or pause for a moment to rest.
I'm happy to say that I squander my days
to pursue an impossible quest.

☙

Sir Galahad was one of the knights of King Arthur's Round Table.

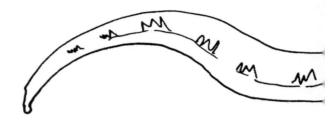

THE SAINT AND THE SKY SERPENT

Lavinia Singer

The next time you feel language fail,
a come-back sticks in the cave of your throat
or splits in a puff of hot air, remember
the stories of those silent in victory.

Take Saint Margaret of Antioch, a girl
of fifteen, whom the Governor of Rome
claimed as his wife. A lionhearted General,
a man of renown, a pagan… She said no.

The thunderstruck man and her father
raged; they conducted such punishments
of torture and scorn that Satan himself
came to swallow her whole!

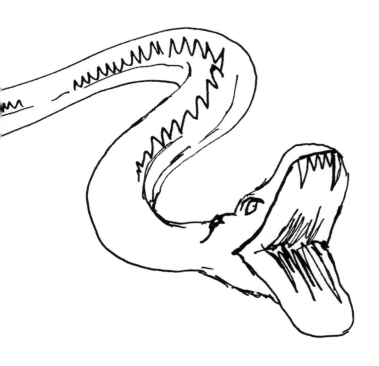

In the guise of a serpent, he swept from the sky
to gulp the girl in a single O jaw-stretch,
her world eclipsed by the moon of his belly,
and choked in obliterating stink.

But for all this, she did not falter one jot.
Raising her forefinger, shake-free, she traced
two lines, crossed, on the sticky skin; and like magic
his innards burst apart, restoring her to light.

ᘒ

Icarus's father was Daedalus, who designed the famous Labyrinth on the island of Crete. Turn to pages 1 and 86 to find out who – or what – lived in the middle of the Labryrinth…

FEATHERS AND WAX

Rachael M Nicholas

With the sun on his skin and the wind in his hair,
Icarus strapped on his wings,
while his father – the wily inventor –
explained some significant things:

Don't fly too high, said his father,
and mind you don't sink down too low.
The sun is so hot, and the sea is so damp
– in the middle is where you must go.

These wings are my finest invention.
They'll fly us to safety, you'll see.
But Icarus, you must be careful,
you must follow and listen to me.

And Icarus *did* try to follow,
to listen and do what was right,
but it's so hard to listen to warnings
when you're taking your very first flight.

Maybe you saw him above you,
soaring and dashing along.
And maybe you heard his loud cheering,
and you thought, well, what could go wrong?

Icarus flew higher and higher,
faster and faster he flew.
He thought he could fly on forever,
and that's what he wanted to do.

His father saw Icarus flying,
and knew he'd forgotten the facts,
that the sea is too wet and the sun is too hot
for wings made of feathers and wax.

Soon the wax in his wings started melting,
and the feathers were falling apart,
and Icarus started to realise
what his father had warned from the start.

And then Icarus knew he was falling,
though he struggled and started to thrash,
and soon enough, poor frightened Icarus,
fell into the sea with a

SPLASH!

The sun didn't pause in its shining,
the day didn't stop being bright,
but Icarus had to stop flying,
and he sank, in the waves, out of sight.

☙

Ginnungagap

Richard O'Brien

Ginnungagap, Ginnungagap.
You don't know what it means.
It could be something beautiful,
or it could be obscene.
It's coming for you anyway.
It fits you like a cap.
You won't know me from Ask or Embla
in Ginnungagap.

Ginnungagap, Ginnungagap.
I'm Loki, by the way.
It's my fault this is happening –
I would say 'my mistake',
but that suggests apologies,
and those are just a trap.
We're heading for a bigger one.
It's called Ginnungagap.

Ginnungagap, Ginnungagap.
I shot the shining god.
In fact, I made his brother do it
for me. Aren't I odd?
I sharpened up some mistletoe.
He popped like bubblewrap.
No other thing could hurt him, see
(except Ginnungagap).

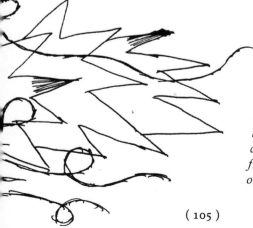

Loki was a Norse god. He
was known as a trickster,
and often his jokes went
too far and had serious
consequences. You can
find out more about him
on page 66.

Ginnungagap, Ginnungagap.
It wasn't for a cause,
or out of jealousy, or hate.
I did it just because.
The tears they shed, and Baldur's blood,
went dripping like a tap
(and don't you *hate* those?), dripping, dripping,
to Ginnungagap.

Ginnungagap, Ginnungagap.
Now chaos comes again,
exactly as predicted,
to the world of gods and men.
A wolf is swallowing the sun.
The stars have turned to scrap.
Don't say I didn't warn you, friend,
about Ginnungagap.

Ginnungagap, Ginnungagap.
The earth's a flaming wreck.
The waters rise to bury it.
You want to know what's next?
I couldn't tell you – there's no land,
no plan, no guide, no map.
There's only everything that's not
and then *Ginnungagap,*

Ginnungagap.

You can read more about Medusa and the Minotaur
on pages 1 and 86.

Medusa and Minotaur Take Tea

Rachel Piercey

The china is in smithereens
before our tea has even brewed
but it hardly matters.
Minotaur is half bull
and a little clumsy
but bigger things have been shattered,
like our reputations,
and we are here with pen and paper
to set the record straight.

We blame the poets
and the storytellers
and the kings playing at war
who wanted this head and that head,
this pesky soldier
and that far-off monster dead.
Often they didn't even leave their thrones.

'I didn't even like the taste
of human flesh, but it was all they sent
into the Labyrinth,' lows Minotaur.
I write this down,
and also that I didn't choose
to have a head of thrashing snakes,
to turn everyone who looks at me to stone.

The poets didn't care to judge
the malice heaped on us
by petty gods,
just how we ended up
and our ability to finish off
their 'heroes' Perseus and Theseus,
men we'd never heard of,
coming with swords and shields to kill us.

Wouldn't *you* put up a fight?
But of course it was useless.
In stories, monsters always die.

I get some sturdier mugs and pour the tea.
My hair hisses and seethes.
Minotaur asks me to write down
that we were lonely.

ഔ

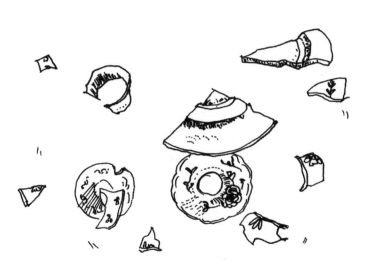

The god Hades snatched the Greek maiden
Persephone out of a field and took her down
into the underworld to become his wife. While
Persephone was gone, her mother Demeter (the
goddess of the harvest) mourned and all living
things began to wilt and die. Nothing grew
again until Persephone came back...

Persephone's Return

Mary Anne Clark

Her mother arrived at the airport early to wait.
She'd checked several times to find the right gate –
Number 3: Arrivals from Hades. She didn't realise
that she was shivering in the air-con because her eyes,
their patient peregrine-power of watching, were fixed
on the crowds that waxed and waned. Like seasons,
  seconds ticked.
And to her the grey glaciers of the airport seemed to fade
and every emerging stranger passed like the shade
of a tree when the sun climbs. With every childless breath
she feared the 'Cancelled' and 'Delayed' like death.
She imagined again and again how her daughter would
  glance
up, her eyes strange and shy as seedling plants.

When it finally happened – when the sun-ray
of that known face broke out between the strangers' grey –
the check-in, baggage reclaim, all, were gone,
and flowers reached the light in the new spring sun.

☞

ABOUT THE POETS

John Canfield grew up in Cornwall and now lives in London. His poems have appeared in various magazines and anthologies and he works for The Poetry School.

Mary Anne Clark studies English at Merton College, Oxford. She has been a prizewinner in the Poetry Society's Foyle Young Poets of the Year Award, Cape Farewell and Timothy Corsellis competitions, and her poems have been published in magazines and the 2014 PBS National Student Poetry Competition anthology.

Joseph Coelho is a performance poet and playwright. His plays for young people have been commended in playwriting competitions and performed at Theatre Royal York and the Pied Piper, Polka and Unicorn theatres. His debut poetry collection, *Werewolf Club Rules!*, was published by Frances Lincoln Children's Books in 2014.

Sarah Doyle is poet-in-residence at the Pre-Raphaelite Society. Her first collection, *Dreaming Spheres: Poems of the Solar System* (co-written with Allen Ashley), was published by PS Publishing in 2014. Sarah co-hosts the Rhyme and Rhythm Jazz-Poetry Club at Enfield's Dugdale Theatre.

Matt Goodfellow is a poetry-writing primary school teacher from Manchester. His poems have been published in anthologies and magazines worldwide.

Matt Haigh lives and works in Cardiff. His poems have appeared in *Poetry London, Poetry Wales, Magma* and the

Guardian. He has also contributed to the Sidekick Books anthology *Coin Opera II: Fulminare's Revenge*, a book of poems inspired by computer games.

John Fuller is a poet, novelist and critic. Among his recent books for grown-ups are *New Selected Poems 1983-2008* (Chatto, 2012) and a collection of prose poems, *The Dice Cup* (Chatto, 2014). His three collections of poems for children are *Squeaking Crust* (Chatto, 1974), *Come Aboard and Sail Away* (Salamander, 1983) and *You're Having Me On!* (Laurel Books, 2014).

Anna Kisby is an archivist and mother of three children, and she lives in Brighton, UK. Her poems have been placed in competitions and published in magazines and anthologies including *Magma, Mslexia, Poetry News* and *The Emma Press Anthology of Motherhood*. She was the winner of The New Writer single poem prize in 2011.

Harry Man was born in 1982. His work has appeared in *The Battersea Review* and *Coin Opera 2: Dr Fulminare's Revenge* among other places. His first pamphlet, *Lift* (tall-lighthouse, 2013), won the UNESCO Bridges of Struga Award.

Amy McCauley's poetry has appeared widely in UK magazines and anthologies. Her current project is a collection of poems, *Auto-Oedipal*, which re-imagines the Oedipus myth. Amy also writes plays and is the poetry editor for *New Welsh Review*.

Paul McMenemy is the editor of *Lunar Poetry*. This is his first poem for children.

Rachael M Nicholas was born in Birmingham in 1987. Her work has appeared in *Magma, Gigantic Sequins* and *The Cadaverine*. In 2012 she won an Eric Gregory Award. Her first pamphlet, *Somewhere Near in the Dark*, was published by Eyewear Publishing in 2014.

Richard O'Brien's second pamphlet, *The Emmores*, was published by the Emma Press in January 2014 and *A Bloody Mess* followed from Valley Press later that year. His work has featured in *Poetry London, The Salt Book of Younger Poets* and *The Best British Poetry 2013*. He is working on a PhD in contemporary verse drama.

Abigail Parry worked as a toymaker for several years, and has recently completed a PhD on play in contemporary poetry. She can most commonly be found writing about beguiling animals, unhappy monsters, magic and mischief. She received an Eric Gregory Award in 2010.

Lavinia Singer edits *Oxford Poetry* and works at Enitharmon Press.

Jon Stone's poems have appeared in books of sci-fi poetry, mimicry and formal adventures. He also writes manga mash-ups and odes to Batman villains, and has edited anthologies of bird poems and computer game poems, both published through Sidekick Books, which is run by the villainous alchemist Dr Fulminare.

Kate Wakeling lives in London and is a research fellow at Trinity Laban Conservatoire of Music & Dance. Her poetry has appeared in *The Best British Poetry 2014, The Rialto* and

Butcher's Dog magazines among others. She is writer-in-residence with Aurora Orchestra.

Kate Wise lives in London, fitting poetry in around being a mum to two under-fours. She has been published in *New Trad Journal, Angle, Prole* and *StepAway* magazines and was commended in the 2013 Cafe Writers and 2014 Manchester Cathedral Poetry Competitions, and placed third in the 2014 Ware Poets competition.

Andrew Wynn Owen studies English Literature at Magdalen College, Oxford. His first pamphlet, *Raspberries for the Ferry,* was published by the Emma Press in 2014. Also in 2014, he was awarded Oxford University's Newdigate and Lord Alfred Douglas prizes for poetry.

ABOUT THE EDITORS

Rachel Piercey is a former editor at *The Cadaverine* magazine and a current editor at the Emma Press. She studied English Literature at St Hugh's College, Oxford, where she won the Newdigate Prize in 2008. Her illustrated pamphlet of love poems, *The Flower and the Plough*, was published by the Emma Press in 2013 and her second pamphlet, *Rivers Wanted*, in 2014.

Emma Wright runs the Emma Press. After studying Classics at Brasenose College, Oxford, she did various odd jobs and ended up working in ebook production at Orion Publishing Group. She left in 2012 to follow her dreams and start a small publishing house. She lives in Birmingham.

The Emma Press

small press, big dreams

The Emma Press is an independent publisher dedicated to producing beautiful, thought-provoking books. It was founded in 2012 in Winnersh by Emma Wright and is now based in Birmingham. The Press was shortlisted for the Michael Marks Award for poetry pamphlet publishers in both 2014 and 2015.

Our current publishing programme features a mixture of themed poetry anthologies and single-author poetry and prose pamphlets, with an ongoing engagement with the works of the Roman poet Ovid.

You can sign up to the Emma Press newsletter to hear about all our upcoming calls for submissions as well as our events and publications. You can purchase our books and stationery in our online shop.

http://theemmapress.com